For everyone that helped me intentionally

and unintentionally on my path for healing.

# Maladaptive Coping Tools

### Not A Therapeutic Book

## Lucky Smith

# CONTENTS

10. Stay

11. My Fucking Reality

12. The Rainbow After The Storm

13. I Can't Avoid

14. Terrible Addiction

15. The Hunger

16. Now I Am Ready

17. Not My War

18. Fair Warning

19. Pathetic Train Wreck

20. Emotional Evolution

21. No One Can Help You

22. All She Ever Wanted

23. Burden Me

24. Thank You Fall Back Plan

25. War On Women

26. I Just Miss You

27. When It's No Longer Fun

28. The Aftermath of You

# INTRODUCTION

## Hello Reader

Thank you for purchasing my book of poems. My road of recovery from using maladaptive coping tools for my life has been a rough road. Life itself can be painful and the tools I was given were maladaptive coping tools. Nonetheless life and the emotions that comes makes the pain a bridge to appreciating joy love and happiness. This book is a small snapshot into my life soul and heart. To be honest everyone and I mean everyone uses unhealthy coping tools in life for one reason or another. However how much or many unhealthy coping tools can be minimized. The question is the quality of life an individual chooses to have for themselves. The last poem has contents of sexual assault that may be triggering for some to read.

## LAST TIME I TRIED

My car was speeding up tires hugging the curvy roads of Azusa Canyon. Accelerating past 30 mph to

40 60 and 90 mph. Flashing in my mind was my entire life. Not very many places I've traveled to my childhood the rapes the creepy old people and countless beatings. Slamming the gas petal to the floor my heart racing with the car. I was so high I couldn't take any more meth into my body. At first I was in-love then chase after that utopia high again and now drown by it.  It was everywhere I smoke it snore it and drank it. I was sick of it making me think and think. Sliding back and forth in the truck was a suitcase filled with hundreds of pounds of meth inside my gas tank and dozens of glass pipes in my glove compartment. Vibrating away was the cell phone resting on my thigh messages popping up on the screen "Where are you?"  Good question where am I? What am I doing? Who am I? Just a 23-year-old drug dealer having a nervous breakdown. It's kind of funny...money's money, right? It's all green. Again the voicemail and texts filled with messages for deliveries parties and celebrities. Here I was on a death wish. I thought money would fix me. It didn't no matter how much of it I made. I thought having fun fucking the hottest people would bring me emotional compensation. No matter how hot the models were or the biggest penis these people were just another item with different price tags. Didn't matter how much shopping buying partying and traveling. None of it matter anymore. Pressing down on the brakes the tires streaked on the road brakes pads digging into the metal and sliding on the dirt

shoulder.  Right before the cliff the Impala stop stepping out and looking at my dream car. I have gotten everything I ever wanted but no idea of what I needed. So here it is do I jump go on the run or turn myself in? Standing on the edge of the cliff watching the river dancing on the rocks. I grab the pipes and thrown them into the river. Today will not be the day I was going to die. That was the last time I tried to kill myself.

# DEATH

Do not leave me in death
Tears that do not dry
Do not steal my soul
Do not invade my dreams

Do not break my spirit
If you must leave
Do it with goodbye
But you cannot deny me
The opportunity
To see you happy
To hope for you to live
To love again
To begin again
Do not leave me in death

# HAVE YOU EVER?

Have you ever
Had that soul shaking orgasm
Muscle spasms head jerking body collapsing
Your inner goddess screaming
Unable to move
So you hold on hoping he'll stay the night

Have you ever?
Had him leaving you shaking so hard
Everything logical you disregard
Have you ever
Had that crazy having sex
Has you wet with just a text
His pheromones surrounds you
So, you peruse him
craving him for just once more
You are counting the day that he knocks on your
door
Have you ever
Deep down knowing this is toxic
His penis hypnotic
He has become an addiction

An additional affliction
To another issue
Adding to your scar tissue
Have you ever?

## YOU ARE MY COULD HAVE BEEN

You are my could have been

You still are my everything
We ended before we could have begin
You are my beautiful black queen
Your coco brown skin
That glistens in the sun
Your soft curly hair
With endless spiral curls
Sometimes I can't help but to stare
At the natural beauty of you
An open heart looking for
What I refused to give
Grieving lost love
Remembering when you let me in
Tasting your tongue in my mouth
Your hands against my back
Between your legs I found paradise
Moments that I cherish forever
Whenever I drift back in time
Wishing to a nonexistent time
That you were mine
I've search thousands of porn sites
Thousands of videos
Hunting for a version of you
Craving for your moans
None of them are you
Your smile that lights up my darkest days
It's my soul that aches for you
Destiny delays
Taking us on separate ways
You will always be my could have been

As you are my everything


# HATE MYSELF MOST


Hating myself most when falling in-love
Hating the vulnerability
Hating the intimacy
Hating the naked truth of me
Hating the promise
Hating the hope
Hating the dream
Hating the joy
Dreading the disappointments

Dreading the day, it all goes away
Like the sunset that slowly disappears

# THE PERFECT BOYFRIEND

The perfect boyfriend
He's not real
You are not real
It's only a piece
The best part
The best part Parttime
But it's the fantasy that I partake in
God, does it sink in
the smell of you
The taste of you
Lusting for more
But it's not real
It's not always the first dates
Never being late
The long deep body shaking orgasms
Craving for more
Setting the bar so high
That no one else can redefine
But none of this is real

# IN THAT MOMENT

Lies are undiscovered
In that moment
Intimacy is replaced by company
In that moment
Sex is substituted for love
In that moment
Love is defined
In that moment
We are fine.
Outside that moment
Knocks reality
Outside that moment
Follows envy and agony

Outside of that moment
Your broken
Outside of that moment
I know I can't fix you
Outside of that moment
You're hurt
Outside of that moment
I can't heal you
Outside of that moment
Your desperate
Outside of that moment
Your reflection you hate
Outside of that moment
Your gone.

CONFORMITY
Inside the studio apartment

After I clock out of my department
I watch him out of the window
He's waiting at the bus stop
Agency robbed from us
Stolen opportunities of me
How can I miss something?
I never had never was or could be
Maybe this is happy
Normal conformed and obedient
We are all well trained animals
Sociopaths' monsters
Just comply
And everything we deny
We are already dead waiting to die
He pulls out his cell phone
It must be someone texting come home
Or is it another reminder he's alone?
The rain is pouring down
He's getting soak
I stop watching TV
Another way for them to watch me
My eyes are free
They can't control what I see
Every day at 6pm he's waiting at the bus stop
We are all slaves to the have nots
He's sitting on the painted metal bench
Lighting strikes about 50ft away
He turns around and jumps
The sign of relief he's not harm
Dropping his head into his hands

He's crying
Why is he crying?
The strangest thing happens
He throws his briefcase into the street
Now he's screaming
Wow the bravery to be crazy
The normalcy squad will be here soon
I should stop watching
His crazy is addicting
What will happen next?
Now he's dancing in the rain
The rage of his passion and pain
Almost erotic so wild and free
The normalcy squad is going to come soon
He knows his own doom
In the mist of his maddest
Our eyes locked
No this is becoming dangerous
I have to be cautious
I shut the curtain
A few minutes pass
The doorbell is ringing
It's insanity at my door
Will the normalcy squad smell defiance on me?
Without any credit my stability I finance
Slowly I open my door
Dripping wet he ask me out of breath
Are you tired of waiting for your grave?

## HALF FRIENDSHIP

It's the fucking pattern

Story of my life!

First, I get used to having whoever around

The texts

Hanging out

Then I'm off dating some random

A throw away

Someone I never intend to stay

Soon bouncing to another rebound

A little sad so I start to call

So, I start to share

In time I care

Friendship is building

Really, I'm hoping

Investing

Testing fate

Only to taste

Recoil failures

Caught in the webs of childhood

Drilling recycles falsehoods

Crashing into reality

Tangled complicated untitled mess

I confess none of it is what I sign up for

The beauty of having a back door

It's their sun turning into the super nova

Dashing into safety from the vortex

As the black hole is sucking in

Everything

I'm drifting away into another space

Counting

Pros and cons

I debated with myself

My wellbeing and health

Is my first

Loneliness the constant thirst

Flying into another orbit

Waving farewell to the half friendship I created


## STAY

I don't wanna you
But I love the idea

Of what we could be
The if only
isn't that beautiful
You fill me, I'm full
I enjoy the fantasies
of could be's
the texts and late-night conversations
Brings deep sensations
We aren't being fair
This emotional love affair
it's still cheating
I'm not thinking
We are selfish
It's unfair
I love love
You're close but not too close
The freedom of loving a married man
How he listens and understands
every part of me
It's the lovely bones
romance with safety nets
Swimming with wet suits
fanning the fire
Burning with desire
He can't hurt me
Because he's temporary
I don't wanna you to leave
please don't believe
That we would be different
just another place, new rent

It's the idea of blank spaces
I'm filling in the places
In my world you love me
In my mind you're missing me
In my reality all you want is me
It's narcissistic of me
I'm in lust with the fantasy
But I wanna you to stay
That way you'll never go away


MY FUCKING REALITY

Starring at blank screen,

Starving for inspiration,

I can't think,

I drink,

My imagination has undergone castration,

When my safety depends on who is at the station,

I slam my head against the wall,

Independence ripped from me in my fall,

Banging my head against reality,

Surviving and I'm not thriving,

Bouncing in my head,

My enemy has become my bed,

No matter what I can't sleep,

The ghost chasing,

My souls' shaking,

Smiles comes in falsehoods of alcoholic happiness,

Falsehoods that are shock-waves of another mess,

It's more than the fact that I'll never be the same,

Or looking for blame,

It's the fact that I no longer hope,

I'm the zombie without the dope,

I hate that I have no control,

Nothing can fill the hole,

It's my life, and it's stolen from me,

This is fucking reality.

## THE RAINBOW AFTER THE STORM

There is no recovery without honesty. Honesty, how I missed you. My addiction hid me from you. My addiction to affection, attention and ideology of love. The rabbit hole named addiction, finally appointed my deepest affliction. He was the ocean that drowned all my hopes and dreams. He was the perfect storm that rain manipulation, and confusion. He was the earthquake shaking my confidence and morals. He was the god of abuse, power and control. In his raging company, I couldn't see the exit sign. I lost my mind. Leaving everything I ever loved behind. We met during the road-trip with my addiction to love. I was so desperate for an instant guarantee. It was up to me to be free. It was my addiction feeding the dark void, that no one can avoid. I crawled away from the perfect storm, and I screamed no more. I ran to the arms of my whore. Soon after. I retired my favorite whore. No more, I whispered to my whore. No more empty sex. No more cleaning up another mess. My whore leaves the condom wrappers by the door, as he walks away. Crippled by silence on an empty bed I lay. Nothing satisfies this beast inside of me. Nothing fills this endless void. Throwing up pictures of the perfect storm into the air. The monster never cared. Photographs shatter on the bedroom floor. Captured lies on film. Captured hopes and dreams. For the first time I'm alone. No more, the perfect storm and the whore are gone. Another U-turn after another wrong turn. I blame myself for getting burn. So, honesty I come back to you. Cause without you I don't know what to do. I beg for your shelter. Without honesty nothing is ever what it seems. Without honesty realities are befuddled.  I just got to take one more lightning strike, just one more time, to listen to his lies. One more day for this tragic story of his lies. Slowly the void begins to fill. The hole inside of me closes, as I let go of instant guarantees, ideologies of love and a thousand agreements. After the perfect storm passed over me for the last time, then came the rainbow. At the end of the rainbow is my dear friend. Friend, lover, and kind stranger. Tears in his eyes, he bandages my wounds from the war inside of me. He kisses my scars and holds me. He lets me walk, run and fall. He is a friend, and it is all I can ask for. I was lonely with my whore. Insanity invaded me with the perfect storm. So my friend returns to me. And when I stop trying to control my destiny, honesty brought back sanity. Clarity of reality.  Honesty destroys the aftermath of the perfect storm. After the storm passed there is my friend, and my friend is my rainbow after the storm.

## I CAN'T AVOID

I wrapped up all my hopes and dreams,

Laugher turned into screams,

How did this happen?

Why did this happen?

Two fucked up people together

Couldn't scale the stormy weather

We seeker recovery

the logic is flawed I see

No matter what

Therapy or couple's therapy

Can't stop what can never be,

Our brokenness made sense to me

I gave all I had

So much I'm mad

Obsess with what we could be

Destroyed by what we will never see

Floating on the sea of shame

I am a shell that's cracking and breaking

All I wanted was for him to love me

But

The lies physically set me free

Entrapment by promises

My poetry drives him to drink

I'm sick I can't think

Is he safe?

I scream at myself

Don't fucking care

His love never was there

Is he okay?

How did we end up this way?

I am haunted by the past

My feelings shatter my mask

All I wanted was a healthy relationship

with my perfect storm

No one else fills this void

His memory I can't avoid.

## TERRIBLE ADDICTION

Terrible love. He is sleeping, while I'm crying. This love leaves me in remorse. Every need never met, no matter how much I cried, ask, talk, demanded, begged and attempted to forced. The bed we shared soak with my tears. Drench with broken promises, secrets and lies. I hate him. I hate myself for loving him. His superficial attention, and shallow erection. Every moment another rejection. This nightmare is the non-fiction story I written myself in. The adrenaline floods my brain every time he enters me. Like a shot of meth, cocaine and ecstasy rolled into one. It's a terrible love. Smashing every mirror because I can't stand to look at myself anymore. Turning myself into his emotional floor mat. His voice pains my ears, his befuddled manipulation and the emotional absence. Fuels a rage I want so badly to release. AND I PUT MYSELF HERE! I thought love was enough to rescue the recluse he became. I'm not saving him, but I'm killing me. This isn't love. Now I flinch at any man who professes their love for me, because he made a mockery of love. Calling this monastery between he and I love, is an insult to love. I don't want him, but I crave him. I don't like him. I don't respect him nor trust him. I need him because this fallacy of hope feeds the lie that I'm this superhero. The childhood hero that can dash in and save that family. Then it struck me, that had he been the person he promises to be. I wouldn't want him. As I complain about this terrible unhealthy love, honesty had he been healthy, he would have never been a subject within my poetry. A topic and poems written long ago, just the protagonist changes. Finally, I run from his company, writing a new story line to save me. Detoxing from this terrible addiction.

# THE HUNGER

Underneath me feet the cold sand, hugging my feet. I begin to strip down, unbuttoning my shirt, sliding it off me, unhooking my bra, dropping it to the sand. Inhaling the cool California wind. The gray waves crashing against the pebble shores. Taking off my jeans and underwear. My toes kicking the sand. One last big breath, I pick up my surfboard and start to run into the ocean. Picking up my momentum, the waves crashing against my thighs pulling me into her beauty. I climb up on my board and began to paddle...waiting for you. Waiting for you naked, I'm myself, stripped of my ego, and camouflage of lies. Lies I told myself for so long, that I thought were truths. I see through. The onions of bullshit philosophy and theories of perfected logic. My loneliness haunted me screaming "RELEASE ME! LET ME GO!" She whispered to me, "Let me feel." The cold waters making hundreds of goosebumps. I am waiting for you. You who I have been so afraid to ride. You my tide wave that may break me. Finally, my only weapon left is my complete vulnerability. I am open now for this last ride...I want to feel you inside the eye. I see you coming, pulling me in thunder the grounds shaking. I know this maybe my last time. You are going to break me. Finally, I am tired enough to scream "BREAK ME. FUCKING DO IT!" At first, I was in control, riding the waves to you. Releasing all the pain, inhaling the salty sea breeze. My last breath before you devour me. So, I balance myself, trusting my feet, legs, and moving with her emotions. Then I make it... into your eye, and I see that monster inside of you. There were hundreds..... generations of alcoholics, narcissists, and addicts. They beat you, neglected, abused, molested, and raped you. Behind them..there you were. That neglected, abused little five-year-old boy. In that moment, I swam to you, trying to save you. But you knocked me off my surfboard. My lungs are filling up with water, I'm surrounded by water. I can't get breathe. Water's going into my nose, inside my mouth, filling my lungs. My arms are trying to swim ashore, but you pull me back under. Finally, I'm drowning. I'M FUCKING

DROWNING! Everything's going black. The lifeguard pulled me back to shore, but I died in that ocean. I am still myself. Then I was awakened, shaking looking at an old five-year-old little girl battling with that five-year-old boy of you in that ocean. It's over I never want to ride that rip tide again. I died that day, and never will I want to save that little boy of you again. I can't save you. I can't save you; you're locked into that rip tide. I died but came back...The hunger to conquer the rip tide is over.

## NOW I'M READY

I thought I knew what love was, but I don't. You have been all I ever needed all along. You have been there for me every step of the way. As I have in the past filled my body with toxins. You cried for me. I called you dumb, fat, ugly, weak and worthless.

Filled you with the shame, I was taught. I chased ideals of perfection, you waited for me. As I as an adult tried to fulfill childhood fairy tales. Regardless, of the reality you hope for me. Never mind the countless times I have tried to delete you from my life. I have ignored you, blocked you and stuff your love far away from me, as I search to fill the black hole inside of me. When you asked for love, I gave you sex. When you needed my emotional investment, I ran away. When you needed my validation, I delivered rejection. You watched as I numb my trauma with numerous of creative addictions. Some of them recycle successful outcomes, and some caused me more turmoil. I guess, I'm here listening, talking and facing you because now I see you love me. It took a narcissistic soul eating dragon, who sucked out my sanity to realize all I needed was you. As I lied strap to a bed, in an insane asylum begging for a cure, you stood by my side. When I had money to burn, you were there. When I had nothing, you were again still there. As I climb mountains searching for a purpose for my life, you trudge along following my every move. I laughed at your feelings, mocked your vulnerability, and belittled your needs. Selfishly, I became the monster I have grown to hate. I screamed at you for feeling, needing and wanting. It took my rock-bottom, to start to appreciate you. I thought I knew what love was, but I don't. I fooled myself into my own image of a relationship guru. I'm sorry for all my cruelty. You are enough, worthy of love, beautiful, smart, and strong. You are perfectly, balanced and flawed. Honesty, as I'm getting to know you, now I'm starting to love you for everything that you are as you are now. Now I'm ready to fall in-love with you. When I say you, I mean myself? I'm finally ready to fall in-love with me.

## NOT MY WAR

Love and hate so close, so strong. I don't love or hate you anymore. Razors of memories are dull. None of it, cuts me. All I ever wanted was for you to love me. You were my fucking god, my world, my hero. All you did was used me. You were my god. God of pain, shame, blame, hate, fury... You were my fucking god. Why me? Maybe I should ask why the fuck not me. How could you do that? I trusted you, I needed you. I loved you. I admired you. You were everything I wanted to be. Now you disgusted me. The most fucked up part of this, you don't know it. Your selective memory, and warp logic. It's tragic. more confusing shit. Hit after hit. Being your garbage disposal stuffing all your insecurities into me. It's kind-of fucked up. Now I attract men just like you. Why did Freud have to be right? Now I'm working towards where I want to be. Far away from your narcissistic personality disorder and every reminder of you. The next guy will not be anything like you. The next guy will be my husband. He'll be my biggest fan. Keep drowning in your own feelings. I will love, trust and respect him. While you're running to anything. I adopted mental disorders that are non-exist to avoid reality. I begged them please let me be bipolar, borderline, OCD something for me to blame. Put a name for this pain. Let me blame anyone but you. But you...Blood test, CAT Scans, doctor after doctor all confirm nothing's wrong with me but a broken heart. My lack of sleep is from nightmares, the traces you left inside of me. Your violence, verbal and emotional abuse. You didn't protect me. Instead, you fed me to sexual predators. As a child every night I wonder if I'm going to die tonight? As a child I wished for death, because I don't have the balls to take your life. As a girl I did to myself what I wished I could do to you. You were my first monster. As a women, you are not worth my life. You taught me destruction and on my own I learn construction. Love and trust are not a disability. Too much fear can be the enemy. My misplace anger now needs to be address. Back to the 4-year-old girl in that awkward dress. My psychologist says, I'm a emotional mess because of you. You're never going to be my savior. I'm breaking the reflection of your constant rejection. Reality is that you did hurt me. But now I'm ready to heal. I'm ready to feel. I'm ready to let promises and lies of you go. Keep eating your own excuses. Your ability for apathy, is astounding. Strip my disguise of anger, I'm just that 5-year-old sad little girl. The saddest part you won't know it. Evolution will bypass you. The most fucked up part is the pain you served is the representation of the battle in your head. It's not my war.

# FAIR WARNING

Fair warning I'm falling in love and you're falling in lust. Fair warning don't worry I'll give you fair warning. Before I'm falling out of love. I can't control the inevitable. Chasing after the impossible. Fair warning soon I will be tired of running after you. Soon the fight will be out of me. Fair warning, I was only dreaming. I was just hoping. Sometimes fantastical daydreams will stop dreaming. Lust will lose its luster. I refuse to march in the pity parade. I'm not mad. Fair warning reality coming. Soon I'm going to get it. We are right now and that's okay. Life is only collected memories. Thank you for sharing those moments with me. One day we will become another nostalgic memory as we grow old in our perspective families. We will wake up to our spouses. The importance of yesterday will pass us by. Just lovers crossing along an academic of how to love. Fair warning don't worry I'll give you fair warning. Before I'm falling.

## PATHETIC TRAIN WRECK

You are a pathetic train wreck,

Bases are loaded your next one's on deck,

I don't blame you,

Logic lost on a fool,

Your so impress with your own reflection,

Self-esteem is not the same as arrogance,

Your lies contains no eloquence,

As you pledge the alliance to yourself,

And you wish for wealth,

Your world is so small,

It will never be a big fall,

Self-esteem built on alienation,

Masturbating to your own impression,

In-love with the hope of your own apparition,


Your nature makes it impossible,

Isolation inescapable,

In the end your will be drowning

In an ocean of misery,

You can't feel remorse, sincerity,

Integrity, and loyalty,

Or love for anyone,

You want everyone,

Logic wasted on a fool,

Your just incapable,

Another label,

You don't know it,

That's the worst part,

You have no heart,

Living on a charade,

In fantasía utopía parade,

Another conquest to feed,

The need of a falsehood image,

Losing the race against your age,

Love me, anyone fuck me,

You cry, beg and plea,

Another flea,

In the mist of your mid-life crisis,

A simplified mess,

You are a pathetic train wreck,

Bases are loaded your next one's on deck,

I don't blame you,

Logic lost on a fool.

# EMOTIONAL EVOLUTION

This is the hardest thing I have had to do. You have been strong, when I was weak. Protecting me, loving me and driving me. You shield me from attacks. My lover, my protector, and my believer. Some say you are my success; others criticize you are my demise. You wrapped up all my insecurities, locking them up. Hiding them so deep inside I forgot that doubt. You were my voice, when I don't know what to say. You were my feet when I was too weak to walk. You were the strength, when giving up was so appealing. Kept me moving, when I didn't know what I was doing. Emotional evolution happens to everyone. I never thought it would come to this. Where I found peace without the fuel of your anger. Happiness, without the cost of someone else. Guilt for the coldness of my past. Traveling to the was in the center and finding the mirror. I looked at the reflection of you. My lover, protector, and fighter. You for who you really are. For all your beauty, pain, hate, apathy and selfishness. Started the emotional evolution. An evolution that started a revolution. A failing battle to where I must choose. So now I'm letting you go my beautiful ego.

## NO ONE CAN HELP YOU

I didn't know that when I met you, I was meeting a perfect god. However, being a mistress to your ego, has gotten old. While I lied to myself that emotional leftovers were enough. Now I'm lonely. All you need is to live in a house full of mirrors. You are your own best lover, there's no room for anyone else. You're right you are in-love. But it's not with me or another woman. It's with you alone. I will not react

TO YOUR passive aggressive bullshit that's not confusing or impressive. But annoying. I WILL NOT LET YOU. You will not be my trigger, invite someone else to your pity party. You have no idea of ABOUT ME. Not that you would care to ask, cause your head is too far up your ass. Apathy unleashes something dark. The dismissal of my emotions and interruptions by your favorite subject...You. Your cryptic generosity laced your selfishness. I gave you my vulnerability and it was used to feed an obese ego. Continue your path to being an narcissistic, no one will have the insulin. Take your head out of your ass and get over yourself, otherwise no one can help you.

# ALL SHE EVER WANTED

She was tall, slender with black hair like cold coals, pale freckled skin but it was her deep hazel eyes, the kind that followed you in a room, screaming a thousand words in her silence. She wanted love, she chases after it, as she was running from reality. I never knew her, I never understood her. All I ever heard from them were stories, about her insanity. Stories about her. The first time, I remembered meeting her, I was 5 years old. I stood in awe of her beauty, happy to finally meet the woman who gave birth to me. I ran into her arms, quickly the monster awakens from his hibernation. I got to talk to my mother for 5 minutes before being thrown into my cage. The monster chased my mother away again. I hated him, he was the soul sucker, feasting on happiness and hope. She wrote, called and she gave me comfort. I feared her insanity, like it was something contiguous. As she loved me, I began to hate her. It was too hard to hate the monster, he was so close. Making him a shadow was easier. She never beat me, but I loathe her arms hugging me. She never screamed at me, or call me names, yet her voice annoyed me, and still every failure... she was the one to blame. It wasn't until her funeral; I learn about her endless giving heart. She was a billboard for redemption, a person who was never greedy, and needy. Often my mother was mistaken for my sister. I hated her. I wish I didn't hate her. All she ever wanted was me to love her. To let her save me from the monster.

# BURDEN ME

Burden me with honesty, Burden me, Burden me truthfully, Dear god burden me, Burden me with your hostility, Don't insult me with falsehood flattery, Or assume that vanity consumes me, Instead burden me, Impress me with honesty, Bravery to vulnerability without guarantee,

Yet the real burden is fear, Fear of stagnation, rejection, affliction, infliction, change. Burdening people with invisible prisons trap within our own minds, nevertheless, burden me freely with love, or better yet let me burden myself to love you. Yes, to love without love being return. Burden me.

Somehow chasing becomes more attractive than living. A daydream lost in translation. The disappearing rainbow, with its fading pot of gold. The next one will be better, the next one will be hotter. Just an excuse to our own self abuse. Just an excuse for us to use. So, I scream burden me with pain. Let me cry, feel, fail and succeed, as I proceeded. Burden me.

# THANK YOU FALL BACK PLAN

I'm letting you go, It's not fair that I'm desperately searching for something better, Leaving you waiting forever, calling after when nothing else to do, calling you my fall back plan, never regarding how your feeling, rationalizing you being my fall back plan. The guy who was my one day and what if, I don't know if I will find my perfect three, but it's not you. We both knew it. There's nothing wrong with you, we just don't not match. You know that, but because of promises you made, you're choosing to wait, out pity or empathy. However, its apathy holding you to your postdated lies. Thank you for the lies, they were beautiful, and sweet. you're a man who deserves better, then to be my fallback plan, you are more than an option, and I deserve sincerity and honesty, where words become reality, living on your lies leaves me lonely.

I don't want to be hoping for an unknown nonexistent idea of who I want to be, while you are in my back pocket as my fallback plan, it just makes me lazy. You already know, I'm not satisfied, not happy with these situations, tired of repeated conversations. Thank you for caring enough to lie to me, thank you for your creativity, really

thank you because some of your lies I needed to hear at a time it was better than reality, I know you would never give up on me, you started to believe your own lies that you were telling me, please no more stories, don't say sorry or that you love me, Be free, I won't make you happy, I'm not your ride, I'm not mad at you, we played each other in reality, we broke away from commitment to avoid resentment. Yet keeping each other in the back burner. While you're sleeping with whoever, and I'm doing whatever. Thank you fall back plan.

# WAR ON WOMEN

## Dear Captain,

Sometimes, I wonder when did the war on women start? I mean think about it, I want to estimate about 60% of men have some inferiority issues against women, disrespect women, and just fucking hate women. They must have some type of loathe towards women, to use women like a public restroom. Talk to anyone male or female, "Well she acts like a hoe and then gets treated like a hoe." But if she doesn't fuck, she a gold-digging bitch. Damn if you do and damn if you don't. Sometimes I want to scream, "Dude it's not the entire female gender's fault that your mom didn't hold you long enough when you were a baby.

Fucking get over your mommy issues asshole." But it's not just men who hate women, I mean women hate women. Hell, I do it on a daily bases, when I refer to the female gender as bitches I AM PART OF THE PROBLEM, WE ALL ARE PART OF THE PROBLEM! The worst group are men who claim to love the female gender but never a second thought as the condom wrapper hits the floor. I love women but use them and walk on their trust like a worn out floor mat. Then women forgive men for these sexual adventures, because he is a man. It's like most women want love so badly, that by any degrading cost we want that fleeting attention that last if their erection. Women can be just as sexually detach as well. Women can lie and cheat. Fuck it all people can be whores, thieves and liars. It's the entire human species.

What would the solution be? Leave the army? But I want to stay in the war of emotional unavailability. Seeking comfort in arms of a soul less man, that only refers to me as another number on his to do list. Rotation of women on his penis. Sadly, I think men like him are the loneliness. Searching for satisfaction in arms of whores, and women who forgot to love themselves. It's somewhat safe because there is no hope. That ending doesn't change. Stagnation at its best. The bubble of emotional-less sex, surrounded by soldiers of warm bodies. But who are the emotional unavailable army really hurting? It can't be each other because the emotional unavailable are dead inside, living zombies. Living zombies have their brains but lost their hearts. All we are killing are the brave ones on the other side who still love, trust and care. Is this our recruitment? To destroy someone's else dream because ours became a nightmare. We can blame it on daddy, mommy, or the babysitter, but it doesn't justify all this bullshit.

Damn now that I see the problem...I must do something about it...the solution. to be emotionally available...to openly, freely, love and trust to everyone to some degree. I know I may get hurt again and again. But feeling is far better than nothing at all. Respect people just because we share the same air. Respect that's going to be hard, when I see through the facade of lies. Treat others how I want to be treated. To walk away from the captains and generals of the emotionally unavailable army. I want to thank you for the shelter. Still, this is my resignation.

Respectfully,

Your former general

I JUST MISS YOU

I just miss you,

Drinking more,

Acting like a whore,

I just miss you,

Thinking less,

No excuses for my mess,

Self-destruction,

A falsehood ego under construction

I JUST MISS YOU,

Sometimes your memory,

Hurts me,

Feeling guilty,

To being happy,

I just miss you,

It's November,

Dreading December,

I love you,

It's all I remember,

I just miss you.

For James C. Roberts RIP

# LEAVING WHEN IT'S NO LONGER FUN

I'm not anyone's savior,

All their fantasies of me,

Are empty,

I can't be no one else but me,

I won't be Pretending,

I refuse to start Lying,

Walking instead of Fighting,

Not looking for an answer,

Not searching for a distraction,

Not digging for a jealous reaction,

Not searching for love,

Or endless one-night stands,

Just the in-between,

Broken he died,

Moving on,

Only reminds me he's gone,

I miss him every day,

There's nothing no one can say,

It's no one's fault,

Life is an endless comedy,

Where the punchline is me,

Tragedy happens by default,

No one's the cure,

Sharing what I can,

Nothing else is the plan,

Nothing more to be done,

Leaving when it's no longer fun.

THE AFTERMATH OF YOU

Staring up at the white ceiling,

All I'm feeling,

The aftermath of you,

Staring at the blank pages of my dairy,

It's beyond being lonely,

You promised me,

I'm so sorry,

Another birthday

without you,

I'm just staring into yesterday,

All I'm Feeling,

The aftermath of you,

Strangers to my heart,

Lovers in the dark,

My life became your screenplay,

I never wanted it this way,

Nothing satisfies,

The aftermath of you.

By: ELK

For James C. Roberts

Rest in peace my love.

# LOVE BREAK UPS

By: Jarvon Michael Greer and Lucky Smith

Love Break ups your poetry stings me like a bee,
your venom racing in

me, tearing a hole that can never be fill blame it
society but we forget

it was suppose to be about you and me two
supernovas stealing space we

get misplace, u say u are born of love, but yet u run
back to pain,

thinking I'm playing gamez, but dis infection of
sensitivity keeps me

trapped so u beat me cause I abused yo love by not
opening up another

relationship dat ended bad was I meant to have love
hook love break ups

love break ups turning me back to emptiness love
break ups love break

ups turning back to emptiness love break ups love
break ups turning me

back to emptiness love break ups love break ups
turning me back to

emptiness turning me back to emptiness turning me
back to emptiness

turning me back to emptiness


## THE MUSE AND THE ARTIST

I was his muse,

Who fell in love with the artist,

But the artist was in love with art,

This fact was the hardest,

He painted me beautifully,

Capturing me,

During the autumn

Trapping me mad,

In the winter,

Seeing me sad.


Danced for him,

He was my impresario,

Never mine,

Drowning in this scenario,

After fall met us again,

This time we would end,

Pitfalls happens,

When lovers are pretending,

To be friends.

I was his muse,

Who fell in love with the artist,

But the artist was in love with art,

This fact was the hardest,

He was once my amore,

and I his muse,

His paintings and photographs left love and sex
confuse,

To no fault of his own,

I loved him dearly,

Therefore I must set him free.


June the sun discovered,

My age was racing me,

I was no longer his muse,

It was clear to see,

Leaving New York City,

My dreams now became distant and silly.

# FIBONACCI SET

We are a Fibonacci set,

With this goodbye,

is my greatest regret,


Infinite possibilities

but this is our reality,

Spiraling,

It wouldn't be so bad,

If the other half of the set

wasn't running away from me,

Or feelings returning,

But this is reality,

our farewells

the spider web,

Caught and sweetly killed,

Now I know how you feel,

Pain is real,

I walked in your shoes,

But returned them back to you,

My Fibonacci set,

In another realm

we are watching the sunset,

Another time

we are strangers

becoming friends,

To lovers,

Infinite possibilities,

but this is our

reality,

Where never

will be

with you and me,

By chance in the multiple realities,

I'm waking up in your arms,

My Fibonacci set,

My saddest regret,

I can wish forever,

But we will never

To be together,

Maybe no matter

what we keep crashing,

So we keeping

on passing,

A lost thought,

Unsatisfied lover's dream,

If words can…

Than a poem, song, novel, or screen play,

I would write,

If there was anything I can say,

To change this reality,

But it's me,

If it's smoking or drinking,

I would end it all,

You asked for 3 days,

72 hours to delay,

This is reality,

We are never,

We will never,

be,

But it's me,

Nothing changes this reality,

You can never love me,

My Fibonacci set.

Still I wish you everything

And I would have given up anything,

Yet this is the reality,

It's because of everything,

About me,

Breaking apart,

Goodbyes departs,

My Fibonacci set,

My greatest regret.

## DEAR RAPIST

Dear Rapist,

God gave me loud ass mouth for a reason. I will not be a prisoner in your prison, and not going to be your victim. I AM NOT GOING TO BE QUITE, I AM FUCKING SHOUTING ABOUT WHAT YOU DID TO ME. I do not fear you. Restraining from taking the law, into my own hands only because I have chosen to be a living example of what I preach. Right now the law is flaw, but as more and more of your victims speak up, it will change and justice will not be blind. I will use every minute of humiliation, and torture that you inflicted on me that night as my life's inspiration to change the current law. Not only to punish you but to help protect others from men like you. I do not sleep. I do not rest. You will be hunted by the law. I wish that everyone you know abandons you. I wish that your own mother denies that you are her son. You should be in prison; you should be feeling what I feel. I wish you flinch every time someone walks up to you from behind. I wish you have days where you just can't get out of bed and face the world. I wish you have nights where you just can't sleep. I wish you feel the burden of shame on your shoulders every time you take a shower. I wish you feel your owns hands on your skin, when men look at your ass. I wish you doubt every time a man tries to talk to you. I wish you question your sanity. I wish that you question yourself, asking was it my fault? Questioning everything you can remember. I wish you lose all your friends too because your just not the fun party girl anymore. I wish you must make up lies and excuses why you can't go to work, because your swallowing bottles of sleeping pills, then you know leaving your only child that way is not fair to her. So you force yourself to vomit, or going to the hospital. I wish that bars, clubs and events put you into anxiety. I wish that you question your career, and time spent on your education. I wish you must tell a million lies why you're late for everything, but the truth was you were unloading your gun. Saying "I am not going to blow my brains out today. I wish that every time you're driving you have to tell yourself, " I won't drive my car off a cliff," I wish you have to deal with your child, who just wants the old you back. And when you're trying to be this best parent, but that night keeps coming back to invade you. I wish you hide in the bathroom crying hiding your tears from your family. I wish you must fake orgasms to keep your partner happy, because now the idea of sex is now dirty. I wish you were me that night. I wish you immortality, and to always relive my anguish.